Copyright © 2012 Hallmark Licensing, LLC

Published by Hallmark Gift Books, a division of
Hallmark Cards, Inc., Kansas City, MO 64141

Editor: Chelsea Fogleman
Art Director: Chris Opheim
Designer: Mary Eakin
Production Artist: Bryan Ring

ISBN: 978-1-59530-566-4
SKU: KOB1036

Printed and bound in China
AUG12

A Gift For

_____

From

_____

How to Use Your Interactive Story Buddy™

1. Activate your Story Buddy™ by pressing the "On / Off" button on the ear.
2. Read the story aloud in a quiet place. Speak in a clear voice when you see the highlighted phrases.
3. Listen to your Story Buddy™ respond with several different phrases throughout the book.

Clarity and speed of reading affect the way Posey™ responds. She may not always respond to young children.

Watch for even more Interactive Story Buddy™ characters. For more information, visit us on the Web at Hallmark.com/StoryBuddy.

Hallmark's **I Reply Technology** brings your Story Buddy™ to life! When you read the key phrases out loud, your Story Buddy™ gives a variety of responses, so each time you read feels as magical as the first.

BOOK 2

Posey
Saves the Day

By Katherine Stano

Illustrated by Maria Sarria

Hallmark
gift books

Just a skip down the sidewalk and past the big willow tree was Sparkle Elementary. That was where Posey went to school.

She carried her schoolbag that was decorated with ribbons and funny buttons she made herself. She loved going to school so she could learn new things. The more Posey learned, the more she could imagine. And imagining was positively loads of fun!

At school, Posey also got to see her best gal pals. There was Tabby, the chatterbox. There was Kit, the bookworm. And finally, there was Fluff. Posey and Fluff were best friends.

Posey's friends were fun and really nice. They knew just how to make her feel all warm and fluffy inside.

One sunny day at recess, Posey looked at her friends. "What should we play? We could be spy girls in Paris . . ."

"Let's be cowgirls," said Fluff. They had just learned about the Wild West—AND, it happened to be Plaid Tuesday.

Posey perked up. "Yeah, we can say things like 'Howdy' and 'Yee-haw.'
What a marvelous idea!"

So Fluff and Tabby turned their scarves into bandanas. Kit found some rubber bands in her pocket and braided her pigtails. Posey got some notebook paper and stickers out of her pocket. She used them to make her very own hat.

Posey liked making clever things. People were always telling her, "Posey, you are one smart cookie!"

"MEOWza!" cried Posey.

"Giddy-up, cowgirls!" shouted Kit.

"Yee-haw!" said Tabby.

Fluff tried to lasso a chipmunk with her jump rope.

The friends ran all over the playground, hooting and hollering.

The girls stopped to catch their breaths. Then they realized the playground had gotten quiet.

Very, very quiet.

They looked around. They noticed the empty swings, merry-go-round, and monkey bars. Posey was really confused.

"Recess is over," Kit said in a panic. "Everyone's gone inside."

"They left us?" Fluff asked.

"We are SO in mega trouble!" Tabby said.

The cowgirls were shaking in their boots. Posey looked around.
What was a girl to do?

"Come on, cowgirls," said Posey. "We'll find a way to sneak back inside the school."

They ran toward the building. But the door was locked. This was very bad news.

"What if we miss story time?" asked Fluff.

"What if we miss music class?" asked Tabby.

"What if we miss lunch?" Kit cried.

Posey's eyes grew humungous. No way would she miss LUNCH! Once, she had to skip French Pastry Day because she had the sniffles. It stunk!

Posey and her friends tiptoed to the window. They saw their classmates lining up outside the cafeteria.

"Oh no!" cried Fluff. "We ARE going to miss lunch. And today is Fish Sticks Day!"

Posey shook her head. "Don't worry, cowgirls! I have a plan."

Tabby snorted. "You have a plan already? Posey, you are one smart cookie."

Posey pointed to a patch of dandelions. "Come on. Let's pick as many as we can."

"Pick flowers?" asked Kit. "Posey, we're hungry . . . "

"Yeah, our stomachs are growling," Tabby continued.

"Just trust me," Posey told them. So the girls began picking dandelions.

When the pals returned to the school door, Posey knocked loudly.

She beamed up at the teacher who appeared. "Hello, Mrs. Kittywinkle. Look, I picked these flowers just for you."

Quickly, the other cowgirls snuck back inside while Posey distracted the teacher. And the plan seemed to be working—hip hip hooray!

After Posey handed the flowers to Mrs. Kittywinkle, she started to skip toward the lunchroom. "Time to chow down!"

"Not so fast, Posey," said Mrs. Kittywinkle. "Were you girls daydreaming as usual?"

Posey looked down at her shoes. "Yes, ma'am. But we're really, really sorry."

Mrs. Kittywinkle smiled. "Oh, Posey. You can dream all you want. In fact, I hope you always do. Just listen for the bell next time, okay?" Then she winked.

Posey was happily surprised.

Back in the school, Posey and the cowgirls munched their lunch. And boy, was it yummy! Plus their teachers weren't even mad.

Posey decided that maybe Mrs. Kittywinkle had once been a cowgirl, too. That thought made her feel all warm and fluffy inside.

Did you have fun with Posey™?
We would love to hear from you!

Please send your comments to:
Hallmark Book Feedback
P.O. Box 419034
Mail Drop 215
Kansas City, MO 64141

Or e-mail us at:
booknotes@hallmark.com